Struggling filmmaker Kristofer Edan accepts a cash pay day to model the leather ensembles owned by recently deceased, celebrated artist Rafael Ortiz at an auction. Kristofer soon finds himself coveting one jacket in particular that has an unusual addition—a sex ring dangling from its epaulette.

When Kristofer wins the jacket in a second-chance bid, he's in for a big surprise . . . the sex ring seems to have an intense energy, that when in use, conjures up sexual dreams and powers that Kristofer never had before. He soon becomes obsessed with the ring and the dead artist . . . painting huge canvasses that people say resemble those of Ortiz himself. Kristofer starts to feel the dead man's presence and senses that Rafael is just as obsessed with him . . . or . . . is Kristofer possessed by him?

The Sex Ring
Copyright © 2019 A.J. Llewellyn
ISBN: 978-1-4874-2705-4
Cover art by Martine Jardin

Published by eXtasy Books Inc or
Devine Destinies, an imprint of eXtasy Books Inc

Look for us online at:
www.eXtasybooks.com or www.devinedestinies.com

THE SEX RING

BY

A.J. LLEWELLYN

DEDICATION

Dedicated to Reggie, who suggested the idea for this book xx

CHAPTER ONE

I stared at my computer screen. I still couldn't believe I'd sat around all day hoping to nab a copywriting assignment. And what did I get? The crappiest one yet.

How to Book Train Travel to Estonia.

I did a mental eye roll and accepted the assignment. Now I had to come up with sixteen pages of stuff . . . about Estonia. Where the hell was the place? I Googled it. Yep, just as I thought. Eastern Europe. I read the Wikipedia notes. Allegedly, it was the hub of social activity in medieval times. Groovy. It sure didn't have much going for it now.

Holy crap. Including train travel.

Ninety percent of travel through Estonia is done by road, although many highways are still being rebuilt since being demolished in World War II.

World War II?

I could feel a giant headache coming on, and it had Estonia written all over it. I cursed my luck. Some of my co-workers had nabbed the plum assignments. It was supposed to be a first come, first serve deal, but how come the same guys got the best gigs week after week?

I swallowed down some cold coffee and eyed the assignments. *How to Book Train Travel to France, Italy, Spain* . . . but not me. Nope. No siree. I got me Estonia.

Many Estonians choose bicycles over cars.

I wondered briefly about the suicide rate in Estonia as I picked up my new sexual wonder toy, my Tenga. My Tenga could cure all my anxieties, all my stresses. I'd never had sex

1

like it, on my own or with another human being.

My part-time job as a copyrighter for a major *ehow* website was damned stressful. I needed that Tenga. People like me sit in our homes and bid on jobs online. We then grab them and put our best, most creative feet forward creating *how to* articles. Trust me to get a *how to* guide for train travel in a country that had none. It was a tricky assignment, and not one I could toss back to the sea. I kept reading as I stuck my finger in the Tenga's cock port. The massage mechanism pulled gently on my fingertip. Man, my cock was getting hard.

Concentrate, Kristofer.

Okay, you could get in and out of the country by train but despite its new prominence as the spa capital of the world for canny Finnish and Russian travelers, Estonia was still a backwards country. Only in the last couple of years had restoration been made to the Tallinn-Tartu, its major highway and pride and joy. And oops, fifty-six people had already died in reckless car crashes on it. That was not a selling point. Heck, maybe it was.

Since my assignment was being paid for by Eurail, I had to emphasize train travel. I also had to make good use of the keywords that had to pop up at least twelve times each in your report. In fact, the company I worked for had a terrific program that counted down the keywords and removed them from your target list each time you used them.

I'd snatched the assignment after weeks of painful insurance and medical *how to* guides. There isn't anything I don't know about chemotherapy and I hope I never have to use this information.

My attention strayed out the window.

My IM pinged on the computer. My editor congratulated me on finally catching an assignment. This one at least was a little more interesting than the last one. *How to open a stuck jar.* Seriously. I had to compose sixteen pages of step-by-step instructions on how to open a bloody jar. I wondered if they had jars in Estonia or if they ate stones.

Well la-di-fucking dah. How the hell was I supposed to come up with sixteen pages on non-existent train travel to and through Estonia?

My Tenga felt nice and warm in my hands. It wanted me. I could feel it. The space-age looking rectangular box with three speeds and an interior the average hooker would die for was a lot more interesting than train travel. Or jars.

There was a knock at my door and I hastily stashed my Tenga under my desk.

My brother Kiel crashed into the room.

"Thank God you're home." He shook his head. "What am I saying? You're always home. Listen, I need you."

"Me? What for?"

"I need you to model for me."

"Model for you?"

"Are you having a case of stupiditis? Why are you repeating everything I'm saying? Yes, model. I want you to come tonight to my big, fancy AIDS benefit and model some groovy clothes."

"At the risk of pissing you off, why do you want me of all people to model for you?"

"You're skinny."

"Oookay."

"Seriously. These clothes used to belong to Rafael Ortiz. You know, Joshua's former lover."

"The artist? But he died . . . what? Twenty years ago?"

"C'mon, Kris. Do it for me. Do it for our people."

The waves crashed outside my bedroom window and all I wanted to do was write, listen to some music and contemplate the ocean. Modeling a dead artist's clothing? Joshua, my brother's boyfriend had been good to me. Both of them had. But I just didn't want to do it.

"I really, really *really* don't want to. I have so much work to do. I just got a big assignment."

"That is such crap, Kris. I know exactly what you were doing. You were playing with your Tenga. That thing'll break off your wiener. How many times have you used it, anyway? It's only good for fifty loads, you know."

I felt my cheeks flaming. How the hell did Kiel know? I'd become obsessed with my new sex toy since it had arrived in the mail, but still managed to get some writing done. Four whole words. I showed them to him on my laptop screen.

Visit Estonia. And die.

"Estonia, eh? You should talk to Joshua. He went there once."

"Really?"

My brother had the grace to blush. "No, not really. I just lied. I'll say anything to get you to come tonight."

"Estonia is a happening place. It has some roads, you know."

"Oh, whoop-de-do. Now, don't be such a big baby," Kiel said. "You're the only one skinny enough to fit into these ensembles. And it *is* for charity, Kris."

Kiel was such a bastard. He knew which buttons to push, how to get me to comply. He'd wasted his life becoming an artist. He could have made a fortune as a high-class dom.

"Besides, you can always come home and play with your new toy. It won't go away. Hey, maybe you might even meet an actual guy and get a date or something."

I stared at him. My last love affair left me standing at the altar. Literally. I was the only gay man in Los Angeles who'd showed up at West Hollywood Park in the brief time frame when gay marriage was legal, only to get jilted.

It had been a miserable experience and one I was not likely to forget any time soon.

Okay, it had been eighteen months, but I wasn't ready yet. And besides, I had at least thirty uses left of the Tenga. I hadn't even tried out all the different gels yet. My heart and my cock seemed attached to the *wild* blend. Now that Proposition 8 had been overturned and gay marriage was back, I wanted to make a legal commitment to my Tenga. It was the most exciting thing that had ever happened to me.

Sighing, I turned to rifle through the collection of leather on the clothes rack that Kiel had just wheeled into my room.

"All of these will go to auction and hopefully rake in megabucks based on the fact that Rafael had been a popular guy on the gay circuit, not to mention a highly successful painter," Kiel said.

I was well aware that the artist's work now went for hundreds of thousands of dollars apiece. Joshua, an older businessman and art promoter, had been one of Rafael's two main lovers until the artist's untimely passing twenty years ago at the age of twenty-five. Rafael apparently had everything going for him. Looks, talent, money, an array of lovers and, it seemed, incredibly good taste in clothing.

If only he'd seen that speedboat coming.

As far as I know, Rafael Ortiz is the only person I've ever heard of being killed by a runaway speedboat on a city street . . . what a freak thing. It came unhinged from the car towing it and knocked him off his feet as he crossed the road.

He had seemed sun-kissed by the gods . . . and then suddenly, it was all gone.

I tried on one of his leather jackets. I'd never owned one, partly because our mother had browbeaten us into not eating or wearing anything that 'once had a face' and also because I was poor. Leather jackets were expensive.

The one in my hands was very expensive and beautiful. I could smell a faint musky, masculine scent. Man, I was being turned on by a dead guy! All my morals flew out the window the second I touched that jacket, though. It was magnificent.

How pathetic that in my thirty-second year on this planet I

now coveted a dead man's wardrobe.

"It's vintage," Kiel said. "They don't make them like this anymore. It's really sexy, Kris."

"Shut the fuck up. I haven't decided yet."

"All right, grumpy pants. Sheesh."

I had decided though, and he knew it.

"What the hell is this thing on the epaulette?" I asked.

Kiel grinned at me. "What does it look like?"

I shrugged. "Too big to be a ring, too small to be a bracelet." I studied it. It looked like it was made of sterling silver.

"You're kidding me, right? You're the king of the sex toys."

"Holy cow. It's a cock ring!"

Kiel grinned at me. "Now he gets it."

"Where did you get all this stuff?"

"Rafael left Joshua everything but only recently, some of his belongings were discovered in an old storage unit up in Ventura. Rafael's other ex-lover, Vincent, had been hoarding it all. Now Vincent's gone and the contents of the storage space have been in litigation between Joshua and Rafael's family members."

I felt a twinge of pain for my brother. Joshua never showed much enthusiasm for Kiel's artwork, yet he'd apparently gone to war over Rafael's.

"Anyway, none of them wanted the clothing. They all want his art. The only one who saw a value in Rafael's gear was Joshua and I'm lucky he donated it."

I glanced at my brother. Two years younger than me, he had fallen heavily for Joshua, but although he seemed to adore Kiel, he didn't really do anything to promote his work.

Kiel didn't seem to mind. In fact, he always said he preferred to keep their work and private lives separate and who was I to interfere? My track record in the love department was dismal.

"And nobody wanted this?" I slipped my fingers through

the cock ring. It felt warm, cold, hard and yielding all at the same time. I suddenly wanted that jacket. And the cock ring.

"Oh brother. If you love it so much, you bid on the damned thing yourself."

Man, the idea of somebody else buying it gripped me with a feverish sense of dread.

"What time is the auction?" I asked.

"Seven o'clock. Dinner's at six. We can go together."

I removed a leather jock strap from a hanger on the rack. Holy cow. This guy had been a naughty boy, that's for damned sure.

"He liked to wear the jock strap with these leather chaps."

Oh, man, I was starting to covet those, too.

My brother handed me a ten by eight inch glossy color photograph of the artist. Oh, he was a cocky son of a gun. Handsome, with dark, close-cropped hair, he was thin, but I could tell he was packing some meat inside his jock. He wore cowboy boots in the photograph and no shirt. His body had been lean and fantastic. Muscular without being overblown. Things had changed in California since Rafael had been the hottest bad boy in town. Today's sexy heroes favored heavy gym workouts powered by crystal meth and steroids.

We could have looked like twins except I wasn't half as handsome and I didn't ooze that sexual shimmer the man did with a slight curve of his smile. I, too, was dark-haired and dark-eyed, but I didn't have that confidence. Or the smile. I tried practicing it.

"What's wrong? Are you constipated again?" Kiel asked me.

Double bastard.

"No. I have work to do."

I was worried now. I didn't think I had the chutzpah to carry this off. I had to strut on a catwalk in this stuff.

"You're a doll," my brother said, ruffling my head. "We'll need to leave at five, okay? I'll come by and get you. Oh, and

Kris? Don't wear torn jeans."

"Torn jeans are all I have."

My brother shook his head. "You are such a fashion mortality. I'll lend you something to wear."

"Thanks."

Since my near-marriage fiasco, I'd been living in Josh's Malibu beach estate. I rented the bottom apartment of his triplex right on the ocean. I had a room with a desk facing the stunning window, a small bathroom, tiny sitting room with a love seat and coffee table, a kitchenette and a loft big enough to fit my mattress bed. I loved the place and paid well below market rate to live there.

On winter days, the surf crashed against my windows. On sunny days, it was just as spectacular. What wasn't so much fun were the house cat-sized rats that lived on the beach and tried sneaking in through the windows late at night.

Josh and Kiel lived in the top two floors, and another tenant, a music promoter we never ever saw, rented out the other half of the ground floor unit facing Pacific Coast Highway.

It was heaven on earth. And now, I had my Tenga and another new potential toy. I studied the cock ring, wondering what it would feel like to wear it as I jerked off with the Tenga. It was an expensive piece, I was certain. Ornately carved with leaves and flowers, it was still smooth to the touch.

The Tenga was a sensational invention. A rectangular box with three different speeds—my favorite was sucking—you stuck your cock into one end after first filling the unit with lube, and the gel of your choice. The unit, once it was in action, gave a three-hundred-and-sixty-degree stimulation around the whole head. You could control the pressure on your cock at any second with one hand. You could increase or decrease the pressure on your shaft and the head. You could go nuts with the damned thing.

It came with three different gels. The *wild* gel enhanced the sucking sensation since it was a sticky gel. *Mild,* according to the instructions, gave the user the sensation of having his cock softly wrapped in a warm, vibrating ass. Hmmm . . . that sounded good, but the *wild* gel had blown my mind, not to mention my cock.

I studied the other two bottles. Mild or real? Which should I try next? According to the label, real was about as close as you could get to fucking another man. Would I give myself the ultimate thrill using the cock ring as well? I tried removing the cock ring from the epaulette. I heard a sly chuckle and stiffened.

And not in a good way.

I glanced furtively around thinking Kiel had sneaked back in here, but I was alone.

There was a knock at my door.

"Kris, you're not playing with the cock ring, are you?"

"No," I lied.

He pushed open the door.

"I know you like it, but it's not yours, sweetheart."

"But me likeey, Kiel."

He handed me a pair of button-fly jeans. They were pretty sexy.

"Wear these tonight and leave the love beads at home."

"But I adore my love beads."

"Yes, but you can't pull it off, sweetheart. You don't have that hippy vibe."

"What kind of vibe do I give off?"

"Stay-at-home sex toy addict."

"Oh geez, thanks."

He pulled the leather jacket off my shoulders and re-hung it on the rack.

"We're paying you a hundred bucks for the gig, tonight."

That surprised me. "But it's a charity event, I'd like to donate it."

My brother looked at me. "You can use it to bid on anything you want. That way you get something you want, if you win it, and we still get the money."

"Sounds like a plan," I said.

As soon as he was gone, I debated over jerking off or making a decent start on my current assignment. Ever since I'd lost my production deal at Fox studios thanks to the writers' strike two years ago, my life has been one long struggle. I'm a writer-director with a pretty good ledger of film behind me but like countless others, as my old Yiddish mentor used to say, *Woik? I takes it where I can gets it.*

And the internet has proved a godsend for me and many of my friends.

My cellphone rang. It was my best friend, James.

"Fuck! I saw you picked up the Estonia gig. Man, how did you do that? I've been watching the assignment page for three hours."

"I kept hitting refresh every ten seconds. It helps to have ADD, and, or an itchy trigger finger."

"Shit."

I could hear James tapping his keyboard in frustration.

"Did you get the Tenga?" he asked.

"Yep, and it's amazing."

James had bought the Tony Buff realistic cock. Molded to the gay porn star's prodigious appendage, we had decided to compare notes.

"How's the Buff cock?" I asked him.

"Christ. I'm in love with it. I keep watching his movies and fucking myself with it." He paused. "Holy fuck . . . a new assignment just came up."

"Get it!"

He shrieked and I couldn't tell if it was a happy sound or a suicidal one.

"I got it!"

"Fantastic. What country did you get?"

"Oh, shitting shit. I got Belarus. I thought I'd clicked Belgium. Where in Christ is Belarus?"

"Right near Estonia. Welcome, neighbor!"

"I think I'll go fuck myself with my Tony Buff cock, then I'll go kill myself."

"Don't do that," I said. "Millions of people want to know how to get around Belarus."

"Fuck you, Kris. And your no-train country."

"At least Estonia has hot tubs and booze. What does Belarus have going for it?"

"How the fuck would I know?"

I stared at my computer screen.

Points of interest in Estonia. You could get drunk on the boozy staple of vodka, have a mineral bath and go hunting all on the same day within a short area of activity. The bus, according to what I read took forever since many roads were still under construction. The official Estonia website encouraged travelers to rent bicycles. So you'd have to shoot something small if you were going to bag a trophy animal. Or, take pictures instead.

My gaze strayed to the link for the neighboring country of Belarus.

"Good news," I said.

"What's that?"

"Belarus has plenty to offer the vodka and pork lover. You sound out of breath, James. Are you okay?"

"I told you I'm fucking myself with my Tony Buff cock. You try taking this thing up your butt. It's a monster."

"Thanks for sharing."

We shared a quiet chuckle and ended our call.

I stared at my Tenga. Oh, man. If ever I needed inspiration, it was now. I prepared the toy with the *real* lube. It was probably as close to real as I was gonna get anytime soon. I used to have such hot sex with my former lover, Natalio, but frankly, the idea of a real guy who could stomp all over my heart had put me off anything closer than an imaginary fuck.

The Tenga was genius. Absolutely genius. I undid my unfashionable jeans and slid my cock into the opening. The machine sucked and grabbed at me as I increased the tempo. Damn. The thing grabbed me all the way. I slammed into it, my balls slapping against the box and I felt my nipples hardening. I tried to imagine it was a man working the hell out of my cock. Rafael Ortiz's beautiful face came into my mind. His smile haunted me. *Cut that out! He's a dead guy!*

My Tenga sucked and tightened its grip on me. I tried to tell myself there were other hot guys I could fixate on. Guys who were alive. Another part of my brain reminded me I watched movies with dead movie stars — both porn and mainstream. The machine began to make a sound like a real man's lips moved over my cock head. I hadn't heard that sound before.

Oh, it was real. And when I came, the sensation was amazing. I sat for long moments, my cock still imbedded, the sucking sound continuing. I turned off the machine and lamented having to leave it at home.

I glanced at the clock on my laptop. I'd fooled around long enough. I had forty minutes in which to make myself look acceptable on a runway modeling leather fashions.

Somewhere in Heaven, I could hear my mom screaming as she rolled in her grave . . .

CHAPTER TWO

It had been so long since I'd gone to any type of social event that didn't involve glory holes and slippery-floored booths that I felt very nervous about entering the lavish Beverly Wilshire Hotel. As an avid movie fan, I was aware that the exterior had been used for the movie *Pretty Woman*. As a filmmaker, I knew that several sets had been used for the actual interior scenes. As Kiel's brother, I was aware that he'd gone through hell with the hotel's catering staff trying to organize the lavish black-tie dinner to benefit two different AIDS charities. I felt protective of him and a moment of pride swelled in my petrified heart as I realized I was here as a participant in this grand spectacle.

I wasn't dressed for a formal occasion, but I had learned in gay circles that the 'talent' of any event was exempt from conforming to code and I was thrilled to be part of that small group. Maybe it was a large group. I noticed a lot of guys weren't wearing tuxedos. My brother wished me luck and sped off to the catering kitchen to deal with a vegetarian emergency.

Left alone, I stood, watching the crowd. I glimpsed celebrities, celebrity wannabes, and a few rich gay folk who donated a lot of time and money to events like these.

"Kristofer Edan?" a voice said.

I turned and found the blond host of a recent TV makeover show blinking at me.

"I'm Trevor, and I'll be your slave master this evening. Say," he said. "You're cute. Someone told me you were really homely, but you're a bit of a hotty."

He stood back, his head tilted to one side as he looked me up and down.

Mortified, I asked who had said a thing like that.

"Your brother, I think." He took my arm. "Let's get you backstage."

"But I'm hungry. My brother said the food was supposed to be awesome."

"Food? Are you joking? You're a model. You can't eat food. Now listen, I hear there's a slippery spot on the runway so I'll show you where it is from the curtains so you don't fall on your ass."

"Oh, my God, Kris. Could you possibly be having a more *Sex and the City* moment?" a voice piped up beside me.

It was James.

"You tore yourself away from mini Buff?"

"Of course. It's not every day the scullery maid gets to wear the leather. Where are you going? Is there champagne involved? I'm coming, too."

He clung to me and the truth was, I felt comfort in James's presence. James had been my best friend since we'd bitch-slapped each other at Oil Can Harry in Studio City over a dance with a guy whose name we've both since forgotten.

"Oh, my God, I think that's the real Tony Buff over there," James said.

"Where?"

He pointed to a tall, handsome Italian man with a shock of long black hair in the middle of his otherwise shaved head.

"No, it's not," I lied. I wanted James with me. No, I needed him. James would calm me down, make me laugh and if nothing else, keep me mildly distracted until my appointment with destiny.

"Are you sure?" he asked. "My dick thinks it's him. My dick is in love with him you know. I'm certain it's him, Kris."

I dragged him backstage where a bunch of models, male and female, were snorting coke off the backs of their hands.

"My diet?" I heard one girl saying, "is made up of crushed ice and cigarettes. I dream of actually drinking a milkshake."

James ogled everyone. He was a damned fine specimen, unfortunately, he tended to go for guys who were unavailable. His most recent paramour was on his third tour of duty in Afghanistan, which is about as unavailable as you can get.

"What is the first thing you're wearing?" he asked me, rifling through my wardrobe selection.

"This one," Trevor said, plucking a tan leather pants and matching zip up jacket.

"Early Armani. Very nice. They make a change from your usual torn jeans," James said. "Now, strip."

I kicked off my shoes and dropped my pants.

"Underpants, too," Trevor insisted.

My God, I'd never worn anything so tight in my life and the crotch of the leather pants seemed very snug.

"No pants line, but I can see the head of your cock," Trevor cooed. "You have a nice big one."

His fingers patted me, like he was patting the head of a pouting child. I felt embarrassed but soon I was getting more compliments and it all started going to my head a bit.

"Nice ass," I heard someone say.

It was Tony Buff. James screamed and tried to follow him, but Buff was busy walking his followers. He had three men dressed in leather crawling along like dogs on leashes. Each of them had plugs in their butts with tails wagging from them.

He emanated an intense charisma. Boyishly handsome, I knew he was into stuff that was on the heavy side of kink, but man he had a way of looking at you, as if for that split-second you were the only person in the world.

"I so want to be his pup," James said mournfully. "He is so fucking hot."

James and I have different tastes sexually. I liked good guys who could be bad. He liked bad guys who could be very, very bad.

Tony Buff passed by us with a smile. I had to admit he radiated a certain sexual ferocity that made me want to get on my knees and say, "Arf!"

"You feel it, don't you?" James asked.

"If you want to go after him, go."

"No. I'm staying with you, but you owe me. I could be getting my bottom spanked right now."

Trevor stuck a small earpiece into my right ear. I'll give you instructions."

"He needs champagne," James said and went off on the prowl. He returned with a can of diet soda, which we kept passing back and forth between us as we peeked out at the crowd scarfing down their four-course meals. I saw Kiel moving from table to table with Joshua, who looked elegant in his charcoal-colored tux. I watched some of the models do their thing on the runway as the third course of what looked like sorbet was served to the crowd. One girl fell twice on the slippery spot, poor thing. The girl behind her did, too.

The crowd was very lavish with its applause. The first girl returned, bursting into tears as soon as she was out of public view. She tumbled into James's arms. She couldn't have found a better safety net.

"Kristofer Edan, you're up."

Trevor's voice came through crystal clear in my ear.

Holy crap. It was my turn. I heard the fresh blast of music. My throat constricted and I put my hand to it, trying to calm myself down. Madonna. I couldn't go wrong with Madonna. I walked down the runway, felt the eyes of everyone in the room on me and I deftly avoided the danger zone. I did a couple of turns and walked back. In my ear, Trevor was yelling, "Unzip the jacket."

I did, turning around again.

The crowd roared its appreciation. I grinned and took the jacket off. I heard them screaming and whistling and then strutted back, the jacket slung over my shoulder.

I changed quickly into my next outfit, the leather jockstrap and chaps.

"Oh, my God. I don't think I can do this."

James stared at me. "Of course you can. Did you see yourself out there?"

"No, as a matter of fact, I didn't."

"Look." He whipped out his cellphone and showed me the footage he had just shot. I looked confident. I had a kind of swagger. Man, was that *me*?

He helped me change as Trevor hollered in my ear.

"You're next, you're next!"

James started stroking my crotch. "You fill that thing nicely, dude."

He pushed me to the curtained partition and I almost fell face first down the runway.

I made it down and back, beset by the urge to whip off the jockstrap and fling my thing around. What the hell was wrong with me? I jiggled my hips, I did a rutting flip of my crotch at the crowd, then turned and took my time stalking back to the dressing room.

Man, I'm hot! I'm so fucking awesome!

These were not my thoughts. Man, what was in the frickin' soda? Was I hallucinating? I felt feverish, and yeah, hot. Maybe I was coming down with something?

Turn around, fool. They love me! Man, I'm hot! I'm so fucking awesome!

Once again, I turned and preened. I kept trying to turn around, but all of a sudden, my hand was involuntarily rubbing my crotch, like I'd started channeling some gay porn star. My hand rose and I stared as it slipped down inside the leather jockstrap.

"Oh, yeah, baby!" I shouted.

I tried to bite my tongue. What the hell was the matter with me? I forced myself to turn and walk backstage. I got back to James who was jumping up and down.

"You were incredible!" He showed me the footage and I felt shame and embarrassment as I watched my own fingers shoot down between the clip of the jockstrap, clearly touching myself.

Man, I was so aroused in the footage, that my dick got stuck. I had been trying to whip it out. *What the hell?*

"I . . . I don't remember doing that."

"You don't? Man, everyone here's asking me for your number. Can I get some of your sloppy seconds? Some of these guys are smokin'."

He helped me on with another pair of leather trousers and the jacket I coveted.

"You can have all the guys you want. Listen, you have to bid on this jacket for me."

"How high do you want to go?"

"I don't care. I want it. I must have it."

"Relax," he said as my fingers gripped his shoulders. "I'm on it."

How did my fingers get to his shoulders?

I was up again, and I strutted down the runway catching my brother's shocked expression. Joshua stood beside him. He smiled at me and I smiled back.

The crowd was very gracious as I removed the jacket, striking a pose. I walked back to the dressing room and the sad news that I had lost the auction.

"I'm sorry," he said. "You're just too good a salesman. Everybody wants whatever you have on your body."

Trying to hide my dismay, I changed yet again and went back out. Back and forth, I finished my circuit, stunned that I had lost the jacket. It was mine. I was certain I was meant to keep it. I'd felt it as soon as I touched it. Outside, as we all lined up for one last pose on the runway, I tried to act happy as we all went backstage and a couple of guys came up to me, asking for my number. I didn't know any of them. I wasn't that kind of guy, but I took all their numbers, shocked that they had showed me such interest.

In the dressing room, I changed back into my street clothes feeling like I understood how Cinderella must have felt when she got stuck with a pumpkin and a handful of mice. The clothes I'd warn had all been whisked away. No more leather jacket. No more cock ring.

The magic moment was over.

"Wanna go check out the dining room?" James asked me. "Kiel just called. He said they're holding cake and coffee for us."

We went out and my brother and his lover thanked me for a job well done. I was focused on the tiramisu. I wolfed down my own portion, eyeing my brother's.

"Go for it," he said. I sipped coffee and felt Joshua's gaze on my face.

"Have you ever seen footage of Rafael?" he asked me.

"No. I've seen a photo. He was a very handsome man."

Joshua nodded. "I swear, somehow you captured his walk . . . his bravado tonight. For a moment, I could have sworn I was watching him."

James had found a couple of cute guys to talk to and then his cellphone rang. He glanced at me as he answered and came right over to me.

"The guy who bid on the jacket can't fit into it. We came in with the second-highest bid. You want it?"

"Hell, yes."

"How much is the bid?" my brother asked.

"Two thousand, four hundred dollars."

I saw stars in my brain and had a moment of anxiety. It was a huge chunk of change for me but not as bad as it could have been.

"That's so generous of you," my brother said, hugging me.

I couldn't stop smiling.

"Yeah, baby, I'm back!"

"What did you say?" Joshua asked.

I looked around me. "Who are you talking to?"

"You. I just heard you say, 'Yeah, baby, I'm back!'"

I shook my head. I'd heard it too, but it wasn't me.

I began to panic. I'd been doing weird things all evening. Maybe I needed to lay off my Tenga for a while.

One of the women working as an auctioneer brought me my jacket. My fingers closed over the cock ring. *It's mine. Mine!*

She took my credit card and returned a few moments later.

"You were wonderful up there," she said. "You were the highlight of the show."

"Really?"

"I was so surprised. Your brother said you're so shy and quiet." She gave a snort of laughter. "Like I always say, be careful of the quiet ones." She squeezed my shoulder and moved to the next table where a guy took possession of the jockstrap I'd only recently been wearing.

"Hey, hotty!" he shouted to me. "I wish you came with this thing!"

I gave him a finger wave, embarrassed as all hell. I'd just realized who he was. One of my favorite gay porn stars ever. My God, what was happening to me?

"Are you okay?" Kiel asked me.

"No, I'm not. I—"

The guy who'd bought the jockstrap came over to us. He handed me his card. "Hey, my name is Jake Dare and I'm—"

Only the owner of the most gorgeous cock I've ever seen.

He was standing with his crotch at my eye level. I was like a dog in heat. I could not take my gaze from it.

"I know who you are," I said. I stopped myself from

saying, *I jerk off to you constantly.* He was one of the biggest gay porn stars in the world. I'd even entered an online contest to win a date with him and was devastated when I lost. I was so mad reading his blog about his date. Now I raked my memory banks trying to remember what he'd said.

They went to the movies. That's right. It was a no-sex date. I think they ate hamburgers. Now he was at my table smiling at me, chatting with me, like I was . . . *somebody.*

Finally ripping my rude gaze away from his family assets, I glanced up at him. He was a big guy, around six four and pure, solid muscle. He had the kind of physique a close attention to a gym workout will give you, but he didn't have the bulked-up look so many guys had. His hair was cut close to his head, cap-like. I'd seen movies with his head shaved, with a crew cut and also with it longer. When he grew it out, it had a curl to it and it was damned sexy. He had the look of a Roman centurion. Haughty, hot, and oh, my God, there it was. That boyish grin. He had perfect, even white teeth and his entire face creased in happiness like everything was a secret joy. I'd seen it on the screen but it was devastating in person.

And . . . he was using it on *me!*

"Aren't you going to introduce me to your friend?" James asked, materializing out of nowhere.

I made the introductions, but I noticed Jake kept his gaze on me. Wow, talk about being good for a guy's ego! His dark brown eyes had the longest eyelashes I'd ever seen.

"You want to have a drink?" Jake asked me. I couldn't respond because I was too busy thinking about the big cock I knew he had hiding in his pants. I was afraid of saying something foolish.

"Forgive my friend," James said, hauling me to my feet. "He suffers from serial cluelessness, but he would love to have a drink. Wouldn't you, Kris?"

I nodded. *Say something, fool!*

21

"You are so hot," I said. *Oh, boy. I am a fool.*

Jake smiled however and took me over to his table, James breathing hard in my ear.

"Oh, man," he said. "Kris . . . we just died and went to porn heaven."

The entire table was filled with hot guys and we recognized all of them.

Jake introduced us to everybody, and even James became tongue-tied.

"What's your pleasure?" Jake asked me.

"You." *Where the hell did that come from? Holy fuck!*

He laughed, however. "That's negotiable, but how about a cocktail for starters?"

"If you insist." I smiled at him. God help me, I felt my lip tilt up into a sexy sneer. *What the hell am I doing?*

He gaped at me. "You're a frisky one. A quick drink then. What would you like?"

"A greyhound," I said.

James glanced at me as Jake got up to find the waiter.

"You hate grapefruit and you hate vodka. What are you doing?"

"I have no idea! I've been saying and doing weird things all night. I have no idea what's wrong with me. James, take me home before I do something really stupid."

"Doll, if spending the night getting royally fucked by Jake Dare constitutes stupidity, I gave you permission. Just this once."

"Don't leave me alone with him," I said, fretting now. I had a wild urge to service the guy right there at the table, under the lovely white starched tablecloth.

"You are such a tiger tonight," James said as Jake returned with my drink. I took a sip and felt Jake's hand on my thigh as the bitter liquid coursed down my throat.

What had possessed me to order it?

"How come we haven't met before?" one of the other porn actors asked me.

"I'm kinda . . ." I was going to say *a stay-at-home guy*. Instead, what popped out was totally involuntary and not like me at all. "I'm here now," I said. "Let's drink to new acquaintances."

We all toasted each other and I felt Jake's fingers stroking against my balls.

"You ready?" he asked.

"Er . . . ready?"

I could feel James' hot breath on my neck again as Jake spoke.

"Your hand is on my cock. I figure you're ready. I know *I* am." What was he talking about? I looked down and almost screamed. My hand was massaging his crotch and man, his cock was rigid in his tight jeans. I'd also somehow managed to slug down my entire drink. I couldn't even remember taking more than my first sip.

"Can I come too?" James asked.

"Abso-fucking-lutely. I love threesomes," Jake said.

James and I looked at each other and grinned. Hot damn!

My brother was shocked when I told him we were going home with Jake Dare. Jake stood at my back.

"Your brother got me all worked up," he said, holding me to him. I felt that massive boner at my tailbone and once again, I was ready to sit up and beg.

"Be safe," my brother said. He took me aside briefly. "It's been a while for you. You got any rubbers?"

"I do," James said. "I always go out prepared."

"Oh, geez." My brother blinked. "You're both going home with him?"

"It looks like a party," James said. "Four of them are taking us home."

"A gang bang?" My brother looked stunned.

"I . . . er . . ."

"Man," Kiel said. "When you come out of your shell, Kris, you don't mess around, dude. Way to go, bro!"

CHAPTER THREE

Jake Dare had your standard gay apartment in the gay capital of Los Angeles. His large two-bedroom apartment in West Hollywood had some fine structural detail, such as a plastered ceiling with a dome motif circa 1940, hardwood floors, the obligatory, expensive leather sofa, indoor palms in obvious corners, and . . . a ridiculously small, yappy dog. I have no idea why gay men favor these tiny runts, but the rats that try to get inside my beach unit every night would consider Jake's dog a good appetizer.

We had driven in Jake's muscle car—a purple Corvette—and James had sat on my lap the whole way. We parked out front and a couple of Jake's porn star friends arrived. Inside the apartment, they made drinks, but Jake made no attempt at social niceties. He took James and me into his bedroom. As his dog went bonkers barking outside his closed door, he undressed us both. James and I stood, appreciating his beauty as we took off his shirt and slowly unbuttoned his vintage jeans around his swollen cock.

"Oh, my God," I said when I took it out. It was nine inches of perfection. I had no idea how guys handled it on screen. Some of them looked agonized, some of them gobbled it all up. James and I knelt on the man's bed as he stood at the foot of it, feeding his cock to us in turn. It was a beautiful specimen. It was the first cock I'd been near in eighteen months and I suddenly realized I'd gladly take ten crappy how to assignments just get near this guy.

Although he let us take turns sucking it, I felt certain he

especially liked the way I sucked him. I felt cock fever grip me as he grew harder and harder against my tongue. He clubbed my lips with his meaty head. He pushed it into my mouth again, but I couldn't take him all, hard as I tried.

"Let's see what you have going on here," he said, reaching down to unzip my fly. He'd done enough threesomes to know how to handle us both. I was aware in that moment that I'd never had sex with James before and it felt very weird.

"Very nice," Jake said, stroking my thickening shaft, but something had shifted. He'd lost interest in me. I could sense it. I noticed the heated way James sucked Jake's cock, taking it all down his throat.

"Oh, man." Jake dropped his hand from my cock and his intense gaze stayed on my best friend. I lay back on the bed, depressed. It had been so long since I'd been near a cock that my skills had completely eroded. How could this be?

I could see road building in Estonia looming as a job prospect very shortly in my future. James and Jake were getting along famously. Jake was getting first class head. I couldn't resent my best friend. He was as hard up as I was. His last lover had chosen serving our country in a dangerous war zone over servicing James. Hell, I could let him play with the porn star. Feeling very much like a third wheel—I was betting there were a lot of those in Estonia—I zipped up my pants and went back into the living room.

The others were drinking and listening to Katy Perry, slamming the singer's music but they all knew the words and danced to *California Girls*. I began to worry about how I was going to get home to Malibu. I'd have to get a taxi. After spending all the money I had on my leather jacket, a taxi ride would be a damned expensive proposition.

I heard James' impassioned cries coming from the bedroom. I couldn't stand it. Jealousy consumed me. I bid the guys in the living room goodnight and I walked outside. On

Santa Monica Boulevard, the street was hopping. Dozens of gay men drifted in and out of the hot spots. I couldn't believe Revolver was still popular. Every single sidewalk café seemed to be filled. I longed to chat, to communicate. I wanted to paint.

Paint? Where the hell had that idea come from? I grabbed the first westbound bus that came along. I'd just spent over two grand on a leather jacket but was too cheap to take a cab home. I grabbed a seat and felt people staring at the cock ring on the epaulette. I shifted so that my hand was against the window and the cock ring wedged against the wall. I closed my eyes. Somehow, my big, glorious splashy trip on the runway had come to a grinding, spectacular halt. I had no idea why. I'd been in bed with a man I was genuinely attracted to, but I'd run from his room like a frightened virgin.

Attention. I love attention. When I don't get it, I do not like it.

I gasped when the forceful words hit my brain. Where had they come from? This wasn't me. It wasn't my personality style at all. And yet, I resented how quickly the porn star had discarded me. At least I got to suck his dick a little . . . I huddled closer to the bus wall when a homeless woman sat beside me, stinking terribly. She asked me for a buck. I gave her two.

"Last of the big spenders," she said and changed seats.

Geez. Even the stinky homeless woman was rejecting me.

It took me an hour to reach Santa Monica beach. From there I walked over to the taxi stand at Shutters Hotel. I was just about to grab a taxi when my brother and Joshua came by in their new Lamborghini and offered me a ride.

"What happened to your hot date?" my brother asked me. I sensed some envy and a little spite because I was home early.

"He liked James."

"James?" My brother turned and stared at me. I watched the view of the ocean emerging to our left as swerved down toward Pacific Palisades and beyond it, Malibu.

I changed the subject.

"Was it a successful night?"

"Tremendous," my brother said, beaming at me and checking Joshua's reaction. My brother acted so insecure around Joshua, who frankly, was kind of an irritating guy. Not only did he moon over his dead lover's paintings, but he was often imperious with my brother. I wasn't sure he really appreciated just how awesome Kiel was. Not only that, but he smoked electric cigarettes. Until I'd met Joshua, I'd never heard of these things but in fairness, they looked like the real thing but didn't smell like it. They released a faint puff of harmless vapor when he dragged on them. My thoughts flickered briefly to James and I wondered if Jake Dare was still hammering him.

At our home, Joshua took his usual ten years parking his car in the garage. The space easily fit two vehicles, but Joshua's car was like his infant, breast-feeding child. He covered it in a special cloth every night, gave it regular oil treatments and I have caught him talking to it on occasion. My brother and I were forced to make do with the street for our parking. Since the ritual of bedding the car down for the night would take at least a half hour, Kiel invited me into their part of the house for a nightcap. Joshua stood, puffing on his cigarette, watching me. There was an odd expression in his eyes. It was the strangest thing.

Joshua was twenty-two years older than Kiel. He was tall, inclined to portliness, but he was attractive, and his steel-gray hair suited him.

"Nah, thanks, sweetie, but I should go work on my assignment."

Joshua looked pleased. He liked keeping my brother to himself. My brother once confessed that Joshua liked to suck his cock and ass for hours. Hey, if I had a man like that in my home, I'd want to stay in bed with him all day, too.

Kiel hugged me. It was the nicest thing to happen to me all night. I knew he loved me. I thought about James and Jake. Man, it bothered me how bad I felt about them.

"Don't stay up too late," Kiel said. "Get some rest." He was such a mother hen.

Until I finished selling the glories of Estonia to the free world, I wouldn't be allowed to snap up another assignment. Dammit. Why did I always get the sucky ones?

In my room, I played the Beach Boys. The song *In My Room* came on my iPod dock and I thought it was apt. I thought back to happy times when Kiel and I and our lovers at the time lived in a house very close to where we were now on Malibu Road. I'd thought my lover, Natalio, was the finest thing I'd ever seen. I'd had a lot of therapy and a lot of discussions with my brother, but I hadn't had one with Natalio. I still didn't know why he'd left me at the altar. For long seconds, I stared at my computer screen. I'd lost my mom, my man and my dog all in the same year.

And then, a big storm hit, and Kiel and I had lost the most awesome house we'd ever owned. We were still in litigation with the insurance company but luckily, Kiel's relationship with Joshua had flourished.

Alone, as I was, in my room, it was hard not to give in to grief. Dammit. I hadn't thought about Natalio in so long. Now, my emotions were there, right at the surface, threatening to break the sea of emotional calm. I toyed with my Tenga. I realized I was thinking about Natalio because I'd almost had sex for the first time since him. I sat back in my chair a moment.

As a filmmaker, I was always asking actors to reach in and pull out an emotional moment that would work in any given scene.

Holy shit. A part of me felt I was cheating on Natalio. A part of me wanted Jake to want me. A bigger part of me knew that something somehow was changing. Even though, technically speaking, I was still in my room.

I toyed with the cock ring on my epaulette and was beset by the urge to play with it. Dammit. I had to focus. Estonia awaited. Broken roads and all.

The sound of scratching woke me, and I looked up, pain shooting across my neck. I'd fallen asleep at the keyboard. One of the ocean rats was at my window. He was doing a bang-up job of clawing my newly installed screens to shreds. I threw a tennis ball at the window, sending him scurrying. He went right under the house.

Man, I'd have to tell my brother they were apparently camping there now. I stretched my neck and shoulders out. A quick shower would help. A glance outside the window showed me it was still the dead of night. Still, I'd gotten some work done.

I showered, threw on pajama bottoms, my favorite attire day and night, and returned to my computer. I was shocked to see that James had IM'd me. I hadn't heard the computer sounds. I read his messages.

Are you there?

Dude, are you there?

Kris? Do you totally hate me?

We need to talk.

The messages had come through at two a.m. It was now four o'clock. I rustled up some fresh coffee and as I waited for it to steep in my French press, I hit him up with a response of *sorry, I was asleep. How was it?* but I got an error message back saying that James was offline.

I had accessed some cool websites thanks to some Finnish backpackers who had some truly unique suggestions regarding travel through Estonia. Many had traveled with their bikes on trains throughout the whole of Europe and mentioned that for a fee, one could get a ride on a cargo train in

Estonia to some rural—in my mind, old and decrepit—parts of the country to unusual, untouristy spots, such as a local brewery which offered free beer tasting.

Booze and guns figured big in Estonia. That might have explained all those car accidents on the new highway.

I was three-quarters of the way through my assignment when James IMd me.

Dude, he is awesome!

Sighing, I wrote back, *Glad to hear it. Happy you had fun.*

I then typed, *In Estonia,*

Another IM ping. I went back to that screen.

Kris, he was so upset you left. Didn't you get any of our messages?

I stared at the screen, stunned. Nope, I sure hadn't. Then I realized I had no idea where my cellphone was and figured I must have left it backstage somewhere at the auction.

He wanted your number and I gave it to him. He wants you to call him. Dude, he's crazy about you.

Wow. James was so sweet. What a good friend. He was trying to make me feel better.

I thanked him and said we'd hook up for breakfast.

Aren't you excited? Man, he went nuts when he realized you were gone.

He did?

I picked up my landline and called my cellphone. Twelve messages. I played them all back. Each of them was from Jake Dare. They increased in intensity. I'd never heard anything so sexy in my life.

Jake Dare wanted me. *Me!*

The last call had come in half an hour ago.

"Hey, Kris. It's Jake. I just found your cellphone here on the floor in my room. Maybe that's why you're not returning my calls."

Did I detect some insecurity here?

"If you are checking your messages, please call me. I

wanna hook up with you."

Did I dare call the guy, any guy at four a.m.?

I called his cellphone number back. He answered on the second ring.

"Did I wake you?"

"Yeah, but it's cool. Where did you run off to?"

I laughed. "I had to get some work done."

"Listen, I need to catch some sleep here myself. It'd be more fun if you were with me. I love sleeping with a man in my arms. Wanna come over?"

I was stunned to hear myself say, "Yes."

Throwing on my new leather jacket, I raced outside and up the stairs to the outdoor parking space across Pacific Coast Highway where my brother and I shared sandy space with our closest neighbors. I jumped in my car and was halfway to West Hollywood on the 10 Freeway when I realized I was still wearing pajama bottoms.

"Interesting ensemble," Jake said when he opened his door.

"I much prefer yours," I said, my gaze taking in his splendid, naked form.

His hand went to my shoulder, toying with the cock ring on the epaulette.

"Come in here with that thing." He drew me inside, one hand on the cock ring, the other fumbling in the opening of my pajama bottoms for my cock. He bent and licked the head before he'd even closed the door.

We kissed in a swift frenzy. Two hard cocks. Man. Nothing like this had ever happened to me before. I tried to remember if Natalio had ever greeted me at the door ready to rumba. I don't think he ever did. I held our two cocks, rubbing against one another as I shuffled inside, Jake closing the door.

I took my mouth from his for a moment.

"Where's your dog?" I asked.

His expression clouded in confusion. "Dog? Oh, that's not mine. My ex's. They've both gone home." He pushed me to the sofa, whipped off my pajamas with a flourish, opening up my legs. The full impact of having an incredibly hot, naked guy kneeling before me and sucking my cock and ass hit me hard. I found myself both wanting and not wanting to come. I tried hard to prolong the pending bliss, but it had been so long for me that I couldn't hold it. Jake swallowed my cock all the way to the base. When I felt my cock sliding down his throat, I let out a yell and came hard. I felt his fingers stroking my ass as he took it all, his caress on my ass heightening the sensation. He released me as soon as he was certain I'd stopped shooting.

"Man, this is how I'm gonna die, sucking a man's cock," he said. "To me, there is nothing I'd rather be doing."

He tongued my ball sac. I was anxious to get my mouth on his cock, but he was having lunch for one and I went along for the ride. His fingers went to the cock ring again.

"Want to have some fun?"

He released the ring and twirled it in his fingers. "You want to wear it, or do you want me to put it on?"

"I've never actually worn a cock ring," I said.

He grinned. "Isn't it about time you tried?"

When he first snapped it around my balls and my cock, the sensation was weird. The tugging and tightness felt weird. Not good, not bad. Just weird. Then when his hand started fondling my balls as he licked my cockhead again, I understood. Each finger stroke felt like a firestorm at my crotch. The fissures of fire shot both down my inner thighs straight to my ass and up my body, nestling in my belly. The urge to fuck was huge. Oh, man, I'd never felt anything like it. Each lick from Jake caused me to shake. I wanted to beg for mercy. I wanted to beg for more.

"How are we doing, partner?" he asked topping my bound

cock with a kiss.

"Oh, my God . . . I've never felt anything like it."

The cock ring seemed to have an intense energy that would blow my mind if I kept using it, I was certain.

Jake grunted and moved in for the kill, sucking me again. The sounds of him alternately spitting on my cock, then taking it into his mouth was a dream come true. I'd seen him do it in movies often enough. There was a moment where he was always one with another man's cock. He took his mouth from me briefly to lick my ass and the underside of my entrapped ball sac.

Sweet relief came when he moved back to my cock. When I came in his mouth a second time, I watched his cheek muscles work and I blew my wad and my mind. All at the same time.

I heard him speaking, but I was lost to him. I'd floated off in some kind of technicolor world where everything was of a brighter hue. I saw the oddest thing. I was standing in a green field of red poppies. It almost looked like a painting. I felt the world standing still. I saw two men in the field making love. I was ever the voyeur, watching them take pleasure in one another's bodies.

Somehow, I knew the moment was illicit. I'd stumbled on a secret tryst. I watched the undulating ass of the man on top. The man beneath him had wrapped his legs around him, moaning, crying out for more. His body had crushed some of the tender blossoms in the field. My fingers reached out. They were fine, papery flowers. They weren't tulips. I'd never seen them before. Their stems were impossibly green. Shadowed in the dell between two massive trees, the lovers went at it and I felt a popping sound.

I opened my eyes. Jake was rolling off me, the cock ring in his fingers.

"You're a tiger," he said. "I've never let a trick fuck me

before. And I *never* thought I'd be saying this, but dude, you wore my ass *out!"*

What was he talking about? I realized then that we were in his bed. The sun was high. I checked the readout on his digital clock. Holy shit. It was two o'clock in the afternoon! I sat up, realizing now that I was covered in sweat.

"You are amazing," Jake said. His eyes looked feverish. "Nobody ever fucked me like that."

I fucked him? Holy miserable shit! How come I couldn't recall this? What was going on with me? Brain tumor? Early-stage Alzheimer's?

He reached out for me, but then he was asleep, his mouth open as if there wasn't enough oxygen in the room. I couldn't stay, much as I wanted. I owed James coffee and I had to get my assignment in by five o'clock or risk having it reassigned and myself relegated to the copywriting scrap heap. I retrieved the cock ring and my cellphone from Jake's bedside, noticed the stack of spent rubbers on the floor and racked my brains. Had we fucked like postal puppies since I'd arrived? I found my clothes in the living room, threw them on and left.

I felt ridiculous in my pajama pants and leather jacket, but hey, this was West Hollywood and probably the least freaky outfit I'd see on Santa Monica Boulevard. I raced home, showered, changed, made coffee and slid into my chair at three o'clock. I dovetailed from my assignment only once to tell James via IM that I'd meet him at Nobu for dinner at seven.

Finishing up my Estonia assignment within an hour, I nabbed another one, ecstatic that I seemed to be the only one bidding on the train travel through Madrid assignment. I waited for the confirmation and almost screamed.

I hadn't been assigned Madrid. I'd gotten Macedonia. I stared at the screen, calling James from my cellphone.

"Hey," he said.

"Hey, yourself. You know, something is definitely fishy."

"Yeah, like what?"

"I just bid on Madrid but I got Macedonia."

James laughed. "Oh, lucky you. That happened to me yesterday with Belarus."

"How's that going?"

"Just turned it in."

"Cool."

"I was just thinking that the only thing I know about Macedonia is the dodo bird and that's extinct," he said.

"Yeah. Thanks for that. You bidding on another assignment?"

"I just got one."

"Yeah? Which country."

"You'll hate me. I got Madrid."

"Fuck you, man. Then you can pay for dinner."

We met down the road at Nobu, snuggled in the corner of a rustic, but expensive section of Pacific Coast Highway. James lived in Santa Monica in one of the last clusters of bungalows hanging onto its hippy vibe on the edge of the ocean. The small enclave once belonged to the movie star Marion Davies who had owned them as part of a now near-mythic gigantic beachfront estate that she'd had built out of her earnings as one of Hollywood's original movie stars. She'd had bridges, a tennis court, an Olympic-size pool and all kinds of other goodies. She'd sold the property to help out her struggling lover, W.R. Hearst. Bit by bit, the estate was destroyed. Most of it was now beach parking owned by the city. The only remnants of Marion's handiwork were the bungalows, which once housed her visiting celebrity buddies right next to what was once her tennis court.

James worshipped his bungalow. I kept hoping somebody would move out of one his neighboring units so I could move in. He claimed to have no problems with mutant rats even though he lived only three miles away from me.

He didn't get rats, but he did get paparazzi and he waged an ongoing war removing them from his driveway as they waited each day for celebrities who liked to frequent Nobu right across the street from him.

We snapped up a table at the ridiculously busy restaurant that was packed out each and every night of the week. It tended to attract A-list celebrities and therefore paparazzi, but the food was so awesome, James and I still came here. Our waiter appeared happier than I'd seen him look in weeks. Of course, he was an actor like every other waiter in California and he told me with breathless joy that David Beckham was in the restaurant with his whole family.

"My dog has better table manners than his kids, but he tips great. You guys want the usual?"

We nodded. We always split an order of ahi sashimi and shared entrees of black cod with miso and the rock shrimp with ponzu sauce. We ordered a couple of beers and discussed our ailing film careers. As a writer and director, I commiserated with James who was a writer who had yet to strike gold. We always said we'd collaborate on something and talked about it endlessly. Something tonight made me feel like we needed to stop talking and do it. Just like the Nike commercial said.

James was in the middle of discussing his latest bizarre idea when I interrupted him.

"Dude. I gotta tell somebody. I'm going fucking crazy here."

"What?" he said. He looked hurt. I knew he was upset that I apparently didn't like his idea.

"I had sex all day with Jake Dare and I don't remember anything beyond him sucking me off. Twice."

"He gives great head, doesn't he?"

James squeezed some lime into his Dos Equis as soon as it arrived, reaching over to squirt some into my beer too.

"Yeah. But listen, something weird happened. He put the cock ring on me. I started hallucinating. I saw this field with two guys fucking and . . . and . . ."

"And what?"

I lifted my shoulders. "No idea. I woke up at two o'clock this afternoon and we were all covered in sweat. He says I fucked him. Can you beat that? I fucked him and I don't even remember it."

"Were you safe?"

"Safe? Sure. There were used rubbers everywhere. But safe is one thing, safe from memories is a load of crapola. If I'm gonnna have sex, sweetie, I want to remember it." I took a swig of my beer. "Especially if I was the tiger he claims I was."

James looked surprised. "Did you pop any pills backstage?"

"Of course not."

He shrugged. "Neither of us had much to drink—you had the greyhound at the hotel but that was hours earlier."

"How did you find the sex with him? Was it good?"

"Holy shit, to quote you, it was fantastic. I think I have a new porn crush."

"No more Tony Buff?"

He looked appalled. "Don't be stupid, Kris. He is like . . . he's a demi-god."

I smiled. "And Jake Dare?"

"A sparkle on Buff's polished boots."

"Hey."

We both looked up. I cringed. It was Buff's sparkle. How much had Jake heard?

His hand gripped my shoulder. "Hey," I said, smiling up at him.

"Don't you ever return calls?"

I stared at him.

"What calls?"

"I've been calling you all night. Well, since a couple of hours after you left."

"Man, I'm sorry. I think my cellphone's at home."

He nodded. "So, I shouldn't take it personally then?"

"Hell, no."

"It's weird. I was just telling my friend about you," he jerked his thumb over his shoulder, "and here you are. That's serendipity, don't you think?"

"Very much so."

"You want to join us or are you on a um . . . date?" His gaze flicked between us.

"No, we'd love to join you," James said. He scuttled over to the other table so fast I almost felt offended. I joined the others, Jake sitting with his arm across the back of my chair. Every now and then, I'd feel his hand stroking my shoulder or cupping the back of my neck.

His companion turned out to be his ex-lover, another gay porn actor who went by Ricky Street, but who said he was retired now and preferred to be called Richard. He and James hit it off and as we finished our meals, I was surprised when Richard picked up the check.

"Hey," he said, "Jake and I had a great day. We just sold a house we flipped. In this economy, it was amazing. We sold it in just nine days."

"Fantastic," I said. I glanced at Jake who felt warm and seductive beside me. I couldn't wait to have sex with him and remember it, dammit. I'd switched to water after my first beer in case I got lucky.

"Where is the house?" James asked. I would have asked, except that Jake's hand had slipped down my ass between my tucked-in shirt and my jeans. His finger ran up and down my ass crack. I felt sweat beading at my forehead.

"Malibu Road, by Winding Way," Jake said. He was a cool customer. His voice was calm, nobody would know he was doing rude things to me, having a private party in my pants. I was the one who was coming apart at the seams. He grinned, as if he had gotten the desired response and removed his fingers.

I swallowed hard. "I lived down there," I said. "I lost my house in the storm."

"Oh, my God. You're Kiel's brother?"

I looked at Richard. "Yes."

"You looked familiar, then I realized you're the model from last night. Not sure why I didn't recognize you. Anyway, he and his boyfriend, Joshua, came by for our open house. We sold the property right next door to the one you used to live in."

Talking about my old house produced an anxiety in me that I couldn't explain.

I was happy then.

With a shock, I realized I'd said the words aloud.

"You mean, you're not happy now?" Jake asked.

"Um . . . yeah, I am."

"Huh. I think you and I need to have some private time. I'll show you happy."

"Yeah," I said. "Do that."

And this time I'd better remember it.

CHAPTER FOUR

Jake followed me home, squeezing his car beside mine in the parking lot. He was impressed when he saw the house, until we walked down the side of the house and he saw my tiny digs. He had to bend his head to the side to enter the room. Thank God, once he was inside, he was able to straighten again, but he was a good sport about it, dazzled, as I was, by the view.

I offered him a choice of coffee, tea or me. He chose tea.

"Too bad," I said. "All I have is me."

He jumped me then, taking me to the floor.

"I feel like I'm in Munchkin land," he said, when he hit his head on my chair leg and then again on the coffee table.

He had one rubber in his pocket, and I wanted him to fuck me so badly I could feel my heart thundering in my chest. He knelt at my head, letting me suck his cock. I enjoyed it, but then he reached for the cock ring.

Jake snapped it on me, and I went nuts, deep throating the guy like I wanted him to reach my colon. My eyelids flew open and my hands and mouth moved of their own accord. *My hands. My hands!* When I looked at them, they weren't mine.

I blinked and closed my eyes as he stuffed his cock into my face. I opened my eyes again. Oh, thank God. I'd imagined it.

He took off my clothes, preparing me for his cock with his tongue.

"Look at you, wicked thing," he said, reaching over and retrieving my Tenga. "Is this thing any good?"

"Amazing," I said, "but I really want you to fuck me."

"What are these gels like? He snapped open the bottles, sniffing.

"Pick one, slather it on me and fuck me."

He cocked a brow in my direction. "You are possibly the horniest guy I've ever met and I'm the biggest sex pig I know."

Jake sheathed his cock, taunting me with it, rubbing the head against my ass and balls.

"Please fuck me, please fuck me," I begged. He ignored me, rubbing his hard cock along my thighs, up against the crease of my ass cheeks, ignoring all my efforts to get that thing in me. He clubbed his cock against mine, leaning down into my body, giving me his face as a small reward. I grabbed his cheeks, loving the feel of the tint stubble on his cheeks and chin. His kisses put me in heat. Kneeling closer between my legs, he slowly began to enter me. The pain was excruciating. I'd forgotten that we'd allegedly been having sex all day and my ass sure wasn't used it. I soon didn't care. The pain blossomed into radiance. I was back in the field observing the naughty tryst. No, no. I wrenched myself from the blindingly bright images to the present. Jake had the loveliest body I'd ever seen.

I touched my tongue to his shoulder as he hit me all the way home. I'd never felt so full, but in my embarrassingly low repertoire of lovers, none of them had anything close to this mammoth organ.

He took my breath away and then some. He fucked me hard and deep, extracting his cock then slamming it home again. I cried out when he took it from me, so he gave me his tongue to suck each time he took his dick from me. It wasn't enough. I wanted that mystical, magical cock. I felt my orgasm rising and he knew it, too. He read the signs in my maniacal eyes and stayed in me, keeping up his aggressive pace as I came. His hand moved between our tightly bound bodies. He fucked me over and over, stroking my cock in his slick grip. I felt his own release swell and ignite deep within me.

I want to paint this feeling.

Shaking my head, I had no idea what the fuck I was thinking. Paint! Man. One whiff of a real prick and I went nuts.

"Oh, you are the best," Jake said. He picked me up as his cock slipped out of me and held me to him. I licked his sweat-drenched chest.

"You got any rubbers?" he asked. When I shook my head, he grinned.

"If we weren't out of 'em, I'd make you fuck me like you did this morning."

He kissed my throat, right at the pulse point, and I wrapped my legs around him.

"Where's your bedroom?" he asked, glancing around.

"Up there."

He looked up. "Are we both going to fit up there?"

"Sure we will." He had to let go of me, which neither of us liked, but I followed him up the wooden stepladder to my bed. We fell on the sheets, Jake holding me to him as he fell asleep. My hand moved to the cock ring. I unsnapped it but held it in my hand. All night, I had the most intense, sexual dreams.

I woke him at dawn.

"We need rubbers. I'm going to the drugstore."

"Bring back some tea bags. Be a good host."

"I'll do that." He raised his face and kissed me, turning over. I couldn't wait to come back and enjoy that perfect ass of his.

It was quiet and cool, palm trees swaying, the ocean crashing against the sand as I cruised down PCH to the pharmacy. I was pleased to see it was open and I stepped inside, looking for condoms. I was waylaid by the crafts section where they had some deals on paints and small canvasses.

One large canvas stood against a stack of hair care products and some half-price nose hair trimmers. It struck me as hilarious and timely. Now I had a porn star in my bed I needed to make sure I looked presentable. I picked up the nose hair trimmers, then remembered I didn't have any nose hairs. I picked up the canvas instead. I bought a set of acrylic paints, a pack of brushes and was halfway out the store when I realized I'd forgotten to buy condoms. I went back for those and some turpentine.

"You're using water-based paints," the cashier said. "Can't you just use warm water to rinse your brushes?"

I stared at him a moment. "No. Warm water can expand the ferrule, causing the hair to fall out." Now how the hell did I know that?

"Oh. So you have oil-based paints at home."

I nodded. *No, I don't! What the hell am I doing buying paints?*

He rang up my purchases. I felt incredibly light of spirit and body as I drove home. The Tenga was good but nothing beat sex with a hot, male body.

At my door, I felt a pang of guilt when I realized I'd come home without tea bags. I felt so bad I left everything outside and went upstairs to my brother's house. He was a tea fanatic. I'd borrow a couple of bags. He wouldn't mind. I had keys and let myself inside. The feeling of space was pure bliss. I'd forgotten what it was like to swing your arms around and touch nothing but air. I twirled myself around and my cock ring fell out of my pocket. I picked it up and rubbed my fingers against the ornate metalwork on it.

Space. Man, I could paint up here!

I ran downstairs and retrieved the canvas and bag of paints. Upstairs, I took a can of soda from the fridge and padded out to the living room. I was in complete darkness, but oddly, I could see. I squeezed paint from the tubes directly on the canvas on the floor.

Maybe I should get a sheet under this or something. Don't pro-crastinate. Do it! Do it now! My fingers itched to paint. They were *dying* to paint. I had no idea what I was doing but light started to come to the sky, faint lilac and pale blue tendrils across a gray haze. The fog here at the beach was always intense, even on summer mornings, but it always burned off by noon.

My brushes kept moving over the hairline of a man's forehead. *Frown or no frown? Frowns are sexy.* I kept painting, humming and singing to myself. As light dawned, I finally stopped painting and sat back on my haunches, studying the end result. I thought it was pretty fucking fantastic for a complete novice, but what did I know? I studied the face, which took up the entire canvas. Who was it? I'd painted him from my dreams.

I rinsed out the brushes and left them in the sink. Once the canvas was dry, I'd take it downstairs. I grabbed a couple of tea bags from the cupboard and went downstairs. Jake was still in my bed and I felt a small thrill. I put the cock ring next to my computer and climbed the stairs. He was lying on his back asleep, a nice morning erection greeting me.

Climbing back down, I grabbed the condoms from the shopping bag I'd brought back down with me and threw off my clothes. He opened his eyes as I sucked his cock.

"Did you just get back?"

"I've been painting."

He smiled. Man, he was sexy. "Painting, huh?"

Jake gyrated his hips and budged his cock back to my lips. I was only too happy to take possession of his beautiful shaft again.

He watched me sucking him for a moment.

"Get up on my cock," he said, his voice raspy with lack of sleep. I rolled a rubber over him and scooted up to his body, crouching over him. He lost no time sticking it to me and I almost howled at the encroaching sunrise. As he powered his way into me, he half sat up, kissing my knees. It was a sweet touch that made my cock grow rigid.

His hand shot between my thighs and he held it in his curled fingers, cuffing it.

"Fuck," he said, he scooted up, throwing me off him onto my back. He steamrolled back into me and my legs closed around his waist. He fucked me until we both came, his mouth glued to mine.

In the waning seconds of our blistering exchange, I felt his cock pulsing in my ass.

"You are amazing," he said.

"No, you are."

"No, you."

We grinned at one another. We swapped tiny, tender kisses. For a big guy, he was one big, sweet pussycat.

"Make me some tea, then I want to get fucked," he said, kissing me.

I ran downstairs and heated some water. He was in the bathroom when my cellphone rang. It was Joshua. He sounded like he was crying.

"Is everything all right?" I asked, alarmed. "Is Kiel okay?"

"He's okay." Man, he really was crying. "We had a big fight."

"What kind of a fight?"

I checked the time on my computer. Seven a.m.

"There's a painting on the floor of our living room. He says he didn't do it."

"No, I did. Sorry. I didn't mean to leave it there."

"Where did you get that face?"

"I don't know . . . what do you mean?"

"You know what I mean. Where did you see this man's face?"

"I didn't see it. It was a kind of . . . dream."

He was silent for a moment. His weeping grew more insistent.

"What's wrong? What's going on Joshua?"

My brother took the phone from him.

"He says that's his dead lover."

"Who? Rafael?"

"No. Rafael's twin brother." My brother sounded rattled.

"I don't understand."

"He says Rafael had a twin and that he had a fling with him. He says that face is his brother. It's—"

"Raul," I said.

My brother gasped. "How did you know his name?"

I'd know my brother's name, asshole.

Choking off a response, I remained silence.

"You there?" Kiel asked.

"I'm here."

"How did you know his name?"

"I don't know."

"How weird. Why didn't you ever tell me you paint? This piece is really beautiful, Kris."

"Thanks."

"Wow. It's amazing. I feel like this man could leap off the canvas and lick my face. He's a horny one."

"Yeah. They both were."

"What?"

"Nothing."

I was aware of Jake being in the room, poor guy was now jiggling his own tea bag in a cup of boiling water. I stepped into his arms and apologized. He ruffled my head.

"You liked my painting?" I asked.

"It's fantastic. He wants to keep it. Do you . . . are you okay with that?" his brother answered.

"Sure. On one condition. Can I come and paint there later?"

"Of course. Wow. My brother the painter. Who knew?"

Not me, that's for sure. We ended our call and Jake sat on

the sofa naked, sipping tea. I sat on his lap, liking the way he stroked my legs and arms.

"I have to work today," he said. "I've got to pick up some building supplies." He drained his tea. "I'd like to see you tonight. Can we have some dinner later?"

"Oh, I'd love that."

"I was hoping to have a quickie, but I'm gonna be late. I'll call you, okay?"

"Okay."

"And keep your cellphone with you, will you?"

"Sure."

We showered together and I sucked him off. He had the sweetest tasting come of any man I'd ever met.

"Now I'm really gonna be late," he said, but he grinned. I played with his cock and ass as he cleaned his teeth with toothpaste using his fingers. He kissed me and I thought how nice it would be to slide between the sheets with him again.

I pushed him against the vanity.

"Oh no, hot ass. You're going to get me in trouble."

He kissed me again, our cocks getting frisky with one another.

"Damn, boy," he said. "I think I met my match."

He left as soon as he was dressed, and I found myself swooning every time I thought about him. I needed to hear his voice and called him.

"Wow," he said. "I was hoping you'd call. This is the first time you've done that."

I felt so unhappy and ridiculously bereft without him.

"Shit, I miss you," I said.

There was a pause.

"You want to share the thrill of shopping for tiles with me?"

"Yeah, actually, I would. There's something I need to know though."

"What's your real name?"

He laughed. "Jake."

"And your last name?"

"You'll laugh."

"I bet I don't."

"Drake."

"Jake Drake?"

"See, I told you you'd laugh. My parents were hippies."

He told me to give him an hour and he'd swing by. I worked on Macedonia travel and as the hour stretched to two, I began to fret. I shouldn't have called him. I shouldn't have acted like a dopey, needy *girl*.

I turned in my report after spending two creative hours coming up with fun stuff to do in Macedonia — there weren't any — and I spent some time on my company's website bidding on assignments. I almost gagged when I bagged *How to Book Train Travel to Georgia*. Georgia! That's easy. Of course, in somebody else's universe, it would be, but I hadn't snapped up the state of Georgia. I'd snapped up the country, as in the formerly communist European nation that bordered Western Asia, surrounded by the Black Sea.

Oh, joy.

My cellphone rang. It was Jake.

"Babe, I'm sorry. I just looked at the time. When I get near tile quarries I get way too excited."

"Hey, no worries."

"I'm on my way, okay?"

My cellphone rang as soon as I ended the call.

It was him again.

"Give me a kiss," he said.

I gave him a kiss. I think that was when he won my heart. I loved that he was a big ol' sexy goofball. He gave me smooches back. Oh, he hooked me then.

"Until I get one in person, I guess I'm gonna struggle along with my copyrighting assignment. I got a beaut. How to book train travel in Georgia," I told him.

"Georgia state or Georgia the country?"

I was impressed he knew there was a country called Georgia.

He was affronted when I said so. "What, you think I'm a dumb ass because I'm a porn performer?"

"Er . . . no, I don't."

"Honey, I do porn because I like to fuck not because I am as dumb as a box of crackers."

"I never said you were. It's just . . . well, most people I know aren't as smart as you. Or sexy, for that matter."

"You can make it up to me when I get there. And hey, you're in luck. I've been to Georgia."

"The country or state?"

"Both."

"Really? What is there to do in the country of Georgia?"

"Well, to be honest, I went there to fuck a hot guy I was involved with and didn't see more than his bedroom and a few potato fields, so I couldn't really say."

Oh, swell.

He blew me another kiss and said he was on his way. A potato field . . . my mind began to wander, and I saw the field I'd dreamed of with the illicit lovers in it. It haunted me and I didn't know why.

There was a knock at my door and certain it was Jake already, I raced to fling it open. Instead, I encountered a distraught Joshua.

He pushed past me and paced my tiny abode.

"How did you know? How the hell did you know about Raul?"

"Joshua. I don't know Raul. It was a face that came to me. I painted it."

"In the dark?"

How the fuck did he know that?

"Um . . . yeah . . . why?"

"You never started painting before, did you?"

I shrugged. "No."

"And yet, you exhibit more talent than your brother who makes his career as an artist."

"Hey, steady on there, Joshua. That's Kiel we're talking about. My brother. And my brother is a fucking angel!"

He advanced toward me and I thought he was going to punch me, instead, he tried to kiss me.

"What the fuck?" I shoved him away from me. "Are you crazy?"

"Oh, God . . . oh, God." He looked horrified. "Please. I'm sorry. Please . . . forgive me." He took off running and I heard a car honking outside.

I picked up my leather jacket, zipping the cock ring into one of the interior pockets. I took my keys, wallet and cell-phone and closed up. My brother came down the stairs.

"What happened?" He looked ashen. "Joshua says you hate him."

"I don't hate him."

"Everything okay?" Jake stood outside the house.

"Everything's fine," I said. But it wasn't. I hugged my brother who looked more upset than I'd ever seen him.

"I'm sorry," I said to Jake. "I don't want to leave him like this."

"Of course you shouldn't. Come on, I'm taking you both to lunch."

We piled into his convertible Mercedes, my brother and I squeeing into the front seat since the back was filled with boxes of tiles. James called as we neared my favorite place in the whole wide world, Malibu Seafood. My brother had to dig my phone out of my pocket and took the call. He arranged for James to meet us there.

At the restaurant, we grabbed the first table big enough for four. We scored big time since there were only five tables outside the dinky shack-style restaurant. Though it was across the road from the ocean, the tables had an outdoor view and the restaurant had the best seafood in Malibu at a poor man's affordable prices. We all opted for salmon and salad, Jake and I waiting at the window outside the restaurant to order.

The wait staff had the personality of prison guards, but they handed over our bottles of water and our bulging dishes with enough charm to convince me they hadn't spit into our food.

At the table, we dug in, James relating a tale about his night out with Jake's ex love, Richard.

"We went salsa dancing."

"God I've always wanted to do that," Kiel said.

"Why don't you?" Jake asked.

Kiel made a face. "Joshua hates dancing."

"Well, we're going again tonight, come with us," James insisted.

"I wouldn't be party crashing?"

"It's not a date. It's dancing. Come on, it'll be fun."

My brother's whole expression changed.

"Fun. Yeah. I'd like that."

"Want to go with them?" Jake asked me.

"Why not?"

I wasn't much of a dancer, but I wanted to dance with him. After lunch, Jake and I took off to check out two more tile places. The second one was amazing. We visited a woman with the incredible name of Hripsime Jones. She pronounced it for me, Hrip-si-may. She was gorgeous. I'm not bi. I'm no switch-hitter but she had an erotic beauty that made you want to be close to her. She oozed sexiness but was utterly serious about her hand-painted tiles. A large black Labrador and a tiny white teacup poodle patrolled her store on Topanga

52

Canyon.

The lab looked embarrassed to be seen with the little yappy thing. I felt sorry for the big guy.

Hripsime seemed besotted with the other big guy, Jake. He tolerated her kisses and hugs, but frankly, I wasn't tolerating her attention to him too well. I realized I was being a jerk. I sensed her loneliness and frankly, I understood her wanting to touch him. I had a hard time keeping my hands off him myself.

He pored over samples in endless baskets, and she pored over his body.

My mind drifted. I thought about Joshua trying to kiss me. I couldn't fathom that behavior and forced the thought from my mind. I started mentally working on my new train travel assignment.

Train travel to Georgia is punctuated by potato farms.

"Babe? You okay?" Jake asked me, a look of concern on his face.

He got up from the floor and I smiled at him.

"Sure I am."

"Isn't her work incredible?"

"It truly is. I am really impressed."

He gave me a kiss, but I knew he was anxious to get back to the baskets and hunt for tiles.

"No two tiles are alike," Hripsime told me as he went back to his pleasurable task.

I was fascinated by the colors Hripsime used in her tile work.

"How did you get such vibrant colors?" I asked her.

"Do you paint?"

"A little."

She suggested I take a seat and pointed me to a section of large tiles.

"Help yourself. Paint something. You can use a whole tile, or you can smash the pieces . . . here, try it. If you want to break something though, please wear protective goggles."

She had a whole room for smashing them on a heavy wooden bench. It must have been therapeutic wielding her big sledgehammer on all those ceramics. I chose a whole piece of tile and became obsessed with painting the field scene in my mind. I seemed to float in and out of my mind and body. I seemed to know I needed textile medium to prepare the tile. I knew my colors, yet I had no idea once again of what I was doing, but the field took shape. Every last detail rose to the surface. The crushed flower petals, the naked men, the trees seeming to fold in on the pair, protecting their secret.

It pained me to create the piece and I didn't understand why.

I stopped painting for a moment and called my brother. He was surprised to hear from me.

"Is everything okay?" I asked him.

"Absolutely. James and I are shopping for sex toys. I just bought a Tony Buff cock!"

"Oh, my God," I said. "What will Joshua say?"

"I hope he's as happy as I am. James says he can't live without his."

Geez, Louise.

"I thought you and Joshua had a pretty good sex life?"

"Well, yeah, he gives me great head, but he can't fuck and sometimes a man needs to get fucked, Kris."

Yes, he was right.

"Via con dios, my darling," I said and ended the call.

I finished the flowers in the field, ecstatic with the precise color of red that I'd mixed.

"That is . . . astonishing." Jake looked over my shoulder. "You just painted that?"

"Yes. You really like it?"

"Babe, are you kidding? It's wonderful. Who is the guy on top? He's got a damned cute ass."

I didn't respond. I was too busy washing my hands. I was also trying to grapple with the fact that I knew now who the man on top was. I also knew I had to confront Joshua. Which meant, I was about to break my brother's heart.

CHAPTER FIVE

Jake was very cool about letting me drive home with my wet tile in his expensive sports car. He went downstairs to my place to wait for me in bed and I went upstairs to see Joshua. He wasn't home.

How frustrating. I let myself into the house and left the massive tile to dry in the kitchen. I wrote a note for him and Kiel but I knew that I'd be seeing Kiel later. I just wanted to explain that the tile needed to dry.

I ran downstairs and found my hot and sexy lover lying on the sofa, his head titled at an odd angle, his legs dangling over the edge. He was right. I lived in Munchkin land.

Leaving him to nap, I got online to deal with Georgia, which, I soon discovered, had plenty of things going for it, such as its tempting meat cuisine. I had yet to make a discovery of the potato situation, but I just knew meat and potatoes went well together.

My cellphone rang. It was James.

"Kiel and I are going to skip salsa dancing," he said. "Do you mind?"

"No, not at all."

I glanced over at my new lover. Should I let him sleep or take advantage of him? Being the horn dog I was I chose the latter and he woke up, a little grumpy but also hard.

"You are so bad," he said. "Shit. My neck hurts."

His cellphone rang as I was giving him some mouth to cock resuscitation. I listened to him having one of those infuriating conversations guys have when they want to convey information without letting you, the listener, understand the information.

"I gotta go, baby," he said, when he ended his call. "I forgot I have a thing tonight."

Everybody was suddenly busy. First Kiel and James. Now Jake.

"That's cool. I understand."

"Great. Hey, when it's over, I'll call you. Maybe we can hook up."

"Sure. I'd like that."

A thing? He has a thing? Why can't he tell me what it is?

"Are you a rent boy?" I asked him

He smiled, getting to his feet and tucking his cock back into in his pants.

"No. But I used to be."

I nodded.

"Does that bother you?"

"No. I have no judgments about stuff like that. I just thought maybe you had a date."

I had the weirdest images of him dancing nude with other men . . . that was it. He was going to a club. Man, how the hell was I tuning into him? I was bewildered by my careening emotions. It was stupid to experience the hurt I was feeling. I barely knew the guy.

"Look," he said, "there's thing at Mickey's in West Hollywood."

"Oh, you mean Cocktails with the Stars?"

"Yes." He looked relieved.

I smiled. I understood. He wanted to go and perform, maybe hook up or whatever without me hanging around. Geez. I had to fall for a porn star. I needed my head examined.

His gaze stayed on my face. "You know I'm semi-retired, right?"

"No, I didn't know that."

"I was out of the skin trade for years. I was doing great

flipping houses and doing well, then the bottom fell out of the market, as you know. I've been back in the business for about a year, but to be honest, it doesn't thrill me. I've done a couple of fun movies, but I've never had sex like I've had with you."

"Hey, that's nice. Thanks."

"Don't thank me. It's true. Nobody sucked my toes the way you did."

When the hell had I sucked his toes? Dammit. Why couldn't I remember?

He touched my lips with tentative fingers.

"I'm going to tell you this and you'll think I'm all kinds of an asshole, but the truth is, I forgot about this gig tonight. It's with a couple of guys I've worked with before."

"Why does that make you an asshole?"

He blew out a breath. "I was about to get to that part. You're a good-looking, wonderful guy."

Oh, shit. That was always the kiss of death in a conversation with a man. I could see myself about to fall off the budding romance cliff.

"I really, really like you. I want to keep that part of my life separate and I don't want anyone else touching you. If I'm on stage getting naked, I have no idea what's going on in dark corners."

I laughed then. It was okay for him to fuck around, but not me. I didn't say anything. I was going to stay home and paint.

"Tell me what you're thinking," he said.

"I don't know what I think."

That was the truth. Something weird was happening to me. I felt like myself, but I wasn't. I couldn't paint, but I could. I had sex and didn't remember it. I was . . . holy shit. Was I possessed by the dead guy? The thought seemed so ridiculous, I pushed it right out of my head.

"We've had a nice day," he said. "I don't want to leave things on a bad note."

"It's not bad," I said. Suddenly words came out of my mouth and I had no idea where they came from.

"You have to do what feels right for you and I understand. It doesn't thrill me, but hey, we hardly know each other."

He looked at me for a long moment. I realized I'd never spoken my truth with Natalio. Man. How could I have forgotten? He always asked me what I thought. What I wanted. I'd been so afraid he'd leave me if I showed my fears and vulnerability that I went along with everything.

"Have fun," I said. "That's what I'm thinking. It's not your fault I'm falling too fast for you. But it *is* my fault if I pretend it's okay that you want your cake and you want to eat it. So eat it, eat all you can. And if you ever decide I can be enough cake for you, give me a call. Because, I really, really like you, too."

"What? Are you fucking kidding me? You're saying goodbye?"

"No, I'm saying, *gvbrdgvni*."

"What the fuck does that mean?"

"It's Georgian. It means, you tear us apart."

"Oh for fuck's sake, it's just cocktails."

"Yes, which you don't want me to go to."

He nodded. He stared at me, as if bewildered.

"You have to admit, what you said is partly true, Jake. I do believe you don't want me to hook up behind your back."

"Or in front of it."

I shook my head. "You have no way of knowing that until you I hadn't had sex for eighteen months. Well, sex with a man, anyway. You want to keep your options open. It's cool. I get it. But me, that's not my thing. I've met someone I like and I want to see if the flower opens."

"Geez. We just came a long way from, *I don't know what I think*."

I laughed. I really did like this guy. I stepped forward and hugged him. He gave me a long kiss. I really hated seeing him go, hated being blown off, but it was okay. Maybe he was tearing us apart. Maybe he wasn't. Maybe I was *Cinderfella* and my glittery coach and footmen had just turned back into a pumpkin and a bunch of mice.

We walked outside arm in arm. He hugged me.

"You're awesome," he said.

"Yeah, you are, too."

I watched him drive away. Man, it had been nice hanging with him. I could still taste his tongue on my breath, and I thought about the last time I'd been really happy. I got into my own car and drove down Malibu Road. There was the house I'd lived in with Kiel and Natalio. It had started being rebuilt. I hadn't been able to face coming here. Not since Natalio left me. Dammit. We had been happy. I was a good man to him, and I knew we loved each other. I wasn't perfect, but who was?

The tears came then. I walked through the wood foundations, the smell of newness assaulting my senses. I remembered my mom's last night here when we'd all made dinner. I still missed her. I missed her every day. The night she died in the hospital I'd gone to visit her. I knew I was losing her. Knew that she'd tried so hard and in spite of everything, colon cancer was taking her from me. She wanted me to get married, no matter what.

I had taken her yogurt, because she couldn't eat anything else. I held onto one of the wooden beams in my old, new house, remembering her final moments. She tried so hard to eat it. I begged and begged her.

She cried. "I'm sorry! I'm sorry."

And then she was gone.

I couldn't feel anything here from the past. Now voices were just memories and they hurt more than a knife.

My mom had struggled to survive because she wanted to

see me married and happy. She'd never really taken to Joshua, but she tried. She tried so hard. She always worried about us. And we didn't worry about her enough until she died. My dad had died two years before her, and she told me she knew he was waiting for her.

"I miss him so much," she'd said.

The sky grew darker and I was stumbling around a half-finished house. It was peculiar that Kiel and I were still dealing with the insurance payout but somebody else had bought the property, and they were building their own dreams.

Time to rebuild your own, a voice inside me said.

"Rafael?" I asked aloud.

His mad laughter rang out across the ocean.

Okay, now I was losing the plot. I drove to the art supply store in Santa Monica and bought more canvasses and paints. Back home, I went upstairs. Nobody was there. My tile was untouched. Where the hell was Joshua?

I took a soda from the fridge and put the fresh canvasses on the floor. I began once again to paint. On my knees, I squeezed the colors. I wanted to paint Jake but what I saw was the damned speedboat. It was coming at me. I blinked back tears. Okay, Rafael was inside me. He wanted me to get the image out. For hours, I worked in the dark and when I was finished, I sat back. My whole body ached. I was exhausted. I had no idea what time it was, but I switched on lights so nobody would step all over my masterpieces. And they were, they were fucking incredible.

Man, I wish I could paint like that. I chuckled to myself. I yawned, stretched and went back downstairs. I washed my hands, stripped, showered, and was at my computer in my pajama bottoms toying with my cock ring. Nothing came to mind. No haunting images. Nothing. There were no plum assignments to be had from my company. There weren't any shitty ones, either.

I hung out on the computer until two a.m. even though I knew no assignments would start coming in until nine a.m.

What are you thinking?

The truth was I'd so hoped that Jake would miss me and come running back to Munchkin land. I heard a rustling at the window. I wasn't sure who was more scared. The rat or me. When he realized I was sitting right there, he took off.

Damned straight.

Tomorrow I was calling an exterminator.

I went upstairs to bed, gnashing my teeth that I could smell Jake's scent on the sheets. I held them to me.

What are you thinking?

I am such a sap.

A clawing sensation woke me and at first, I thought it was a rat. Instead, I realized it was Joshua.

"The paintings." He sobbed relentlessly. "It's you, isn't it?"

I stared at him. My head nodded, but it wasn't me doing it. "What . . . how?"

"I don't know. The cock ring. I touched it and pow! I'm a sex fiend."

"It was his favorite toy. He was very provocative." He swiped at his tears, jabbing a finger at me. "You, I mean. Raf, is it really you?"

"He comes and goes."

"Does he tell you what to say?"

"No. One second I'm me and the next he's saying . . . you know . . . provocative things."

He slumped on my bed. Whatever happened, my brother couldn't find us like this.

I hustled out of bed and down the stairs. He followed me, almost tumbling to the floor when he missed a step. I grabbed him, surprised that he was shaking so badly. I changed into jeans and a T-shirt in the bathroom. It hurt to see the tube of toothpaste on the vanity, remembering how Jake had cleaned his teeth with his finger.

In the living room, Joshua sat on my sofa, looking broken.

"Where's Kiel?" I asked.

"He went to some cocktail thing in West Hollywood."

That took the wind out of my sails. So he and James had blown me off and Jake had too. I might have channeled a hot, dead painter but I was still getting rejected all over the place.

"Let's go upstairs," I said.

He shrugged. He really was a mess.

Outside, we encountered a couple of rats.

"They're getting worse," he said. "We should call somebody about that."

He stumbled up the stairs. He seemed so old and frail. In the house, I surveyed the paintings. Now I was sort of me again, I saw their rage and anger.

"The painting in the kitchen is so different to these. This is more the Rafael I know." He gestured at the canvasses on the floor. "He always painted this way, telling a story. I keep saying he. He is in you, so I should say *you*."

"Do you know why the painting is different?"

He shook his head.

"Rafael is trying to tell you something."

He looked spooked. "Tell me what?"

I walked into the kitchen and picked up the tile. It was heavier than I remembered.

"This is a painting of love. This is you, isn't it?"

The tears came back to his eyes. "Yes, it's me."

"Making love to Raul. Rafael knows you really love him."

I felt something leaving my heart, a heaviness, an ache I'd been carrying with me. Rafael had felt the agony of rejection, too.

"You loved my brother, not me. I saw you. I knew. But I was selfish, and I wanted you. You wanted my art."

"Oh, my God!" Joshua screamed. "Is he telling you to say

63

these things?"

"No, they just pop out of my mouth."

Rafael spoke much quicker than I did.

"Raul is still single. He still loves you. Don't fight over me anymore. I am gone. My work . . . this shit means nothing. Love means everything. Go to him."

"But . . . I'm with Kiel."

"You don't love him. He's not me and you can't punish him anymore because he doesn't paint like me. Release him and let me go, too."

"Raul still loves me?"

"You stupid man! You've wasted all these years. Why?"

"Because I felt so guilty. I felt so bad for cheating on you with your own brother."

Oh, Jesus.

We both fell into wing chairs opposite the sofa. I stared at the images of the paintings. Rafael weeping, Rafael seeing the speedboat. Rafael watching, waiting, wanting to make things right.

"Call him," I said.

"Your voice is different. Is that you or Rafael?"

"Me," I said. "I think he's gone for now."

"Where does he go?"

"I have no idea."

Man, even the dead guy's rejecting me.

"When Kiel comes home, I'll talk to him and then I'll call Raul."

"And I'm gonna get some sleep. Goodnight."

I went back to my room and closed the door. I napped on the sofa. Goddamnit. It held the scent of Jake, too.

My dreams were turbulent. I felt Rafael turning, dancing, laughing. He was mocking me. His face became Jake's. I turned on the sofa, getting a face full of fabric. I opened my eyes. It was seven o'clock in the morning. I changed into sweats and took a run on the beach. When my dog was alive, he ran with me every day. I'd hardened my heart to getting another one because to lose my mom, my man and my mutt, all in the same year had almost buried me. Of all the things God got wrong, letting companion animals die before us was the worst. Maybe I could rescue another mutt. Maybe I should get back to my movie career.

Unless I was hooked on trains, potato fields, and broken roads.

Back home, I showered, changed and made coffee. I caught up on emails and contemplated some of the ideas I'd had for movies. Man, I just didn't want to deal with this shit right now.

I was surprised to look out the kitchen window and see my brother coming down the walkway to my place.

"Dude, we need to talk," he said, when I opened the door.

He came in and sat down on the sofa.

"I'm in love with James."

"What?"

"Come on, don't tell me you didn't notice something going on?"

"No, I didn't. Oh, Kiel I'm so happy for you."

"You are?"

I rushed over and hugged him. "Of course I am."

"Oh, Kris. We were so worried. I know he's your best friend. James was worried you'd hate him. He wants his friendship with you so much." His eyes moistened. "It won't change anything between you, I promise."

I put my hands on my brother's shoulders.

"He's a fine man and I love him. I couldn't think of a better partner for you."

"You really mean that?"

"Have you told Joshua?"

He sagged a little. "No. We have to talk. Ever since we got

hold of Rafael's clothing, he's been a total ass."

"Rafael is a powerful guy. Dead or alive."

"He's a better painter than me. Joshua never stops reminding me of that."

"It's bullshit, Kiel. Your work is different. You're a wonderful painter. You paint with love."

"Thanks, Kris. You heard from Jake?"

"No. You went to Mickey's last night, didn't you?"

"Yeah." He looked sheepish. "How did you know?"

"Joshua told me."

"James and I . . . we kinda wanted to have a little date and see how it felt and oh, Kris, it just feels one hundred percent right."

"I am really happy for you both. You have no idea." I couldn't resist. I really had to know. "Did you speak to Jake?"

"No, not really. He got blasted, boy. He really got drunk. I saw him all over some twink. It was really strange." He glanced away from me. "Sorry, hon. I shouldn't have said anything."

"No, I'm glad you told me."

A twink. Christ. Nothing like me at all. I'm not his type. I don't think I'm anyone's type.

"Say, now that you and James are you know, *a deux*, do you think you could give me custody of the Tony Buff cocks?"

He laughed. "I saw you with Jake. He's sprung. He likes you. He's just . . . you know . . . maybe not ready for you yet."

"Ain't that the story of my life?"

We grinned at each other. I was so happy for my brother and for James.

He left me to deal with his life and I went back to the computer to deal with mine. Being online trying to bid on a job was tempting. I could swing over to a couple of porn sites and ogle Jake. But that wasn't the Jake I was in love with.

Shit. The L word.

I refreshed the bidding page. Up popped some

assignments. They were all kaka. Each and every one of them. I bid on the first one and got a surprise. Train travel to Madrid. I thought James had taken that one.

My editor hailed me via IM and told me James had turned the assignment back in. Man, he'd given it up to spend the evening with my brother. How romantic was that? I hoped he hadn't fucked up his career.

Dammit. We'd both been fucking up our careers. I called him and got his voicemail. I told him I was thrilled about him and Kiel and how we had to start work on a movie.

"Let's toss some ideas around for real," I said. "Call me."

My brother came down again a few minutes later, his eyes red-rimmed.

"Joshua and I have broken up. He wants us to move out."

"Fair enough."

"He's giving us thirty days. He's going up to Santa Barbara to see Raul."

Kiel flopped on my sofa.

"Want to get a place together?" he asked.

"Sure."

A knock at the door revealed an exterminator.

"I'm here about the rats," he said.

"About time too." Kiel led him outside, and we showed him where we thought the rats were coming in and out of.

"There's a lot of feces outside this door."

He pointed to the home of our strange neighbor whom none of us ever saw.

We knocked several times and Kiel tried the guy's phone line from his cellphone. We heard the phone ringing.

"When was the last time you saw him?" Kiel asked me.

"It's been weeks."

"I don't have a key. I think Joshua does. I'm going to ask him before he leaves town."

He sprinted up the stairs and returned with Joshua who

brandished a huge ring of keys. I knew he owned a lot of Malibu properties and had rentals up and down the highway.

Once again, we knocked. No response. He unlocked the door and the stench was unbelievable when he opened it. What we saw was so shocking I don't think I will ever forget it. The entire place was swarming with rats. Big, disgusting, nest-building rats.

"Fuck me," the exterminator said and crossed himself.

I had never seen anything like it. The rats had built a nest out of sheets, pans, pots, hairbrushes, toilet paper . . . you name it, the thing went on forever. I was disgusted and completely freaked out.

The exterminator looked like he was going to have a heart attack.

"I have to report this to the city. This building is quarantined as of now."

"Has he been breeding these things in my house?" Joshua asked.

"Looks like it." The exterminator didn't want to venture inside. He claimed there were busted cages and all kinds of other horrors we didn't want to know about.

"We have to move out," my brother said.

Joshua packed his most vital possessions and left just as the health department officials arrived. There were rats everywhere and all kinds of trucks and even the cops stopped.

"About three hundred rats," somebody said.

I couldn't pack and get out fast enough. I left my furniture and took only my clothes, my laptop, my top sex toys, DVDs and some books.

My brother was moving in with James.

And I was on the prowl for new digs.

"Stay in touch," my brother said.

Yeah. I'd put a call through to James but hadn't even

received a response, but my brother had spoken to him and was moving in. Holy shit. I was losing everything again.

CHAPTER SIX

I drove around PCH looking for new digs. Most of the places I saw were decrepit. One place even had a completely charred kitchen courtesy of the previous drug-addled tenants. It had an ocean-view, was otherwise spacious and, it was rat free. The kitchen was alarming and in spite of the landlord's reduced rent in exchange for my improvements on it, I was not a handyman. Neither, I sensed was Rafael.

We kept moving.

I needed to stay somewhere so I checked into a motel across the road from the beach so I could get some work done. I had a great view of the ocean, even though a road separated me from it. It was nice and roomy. No more Munchkin land. It was a nice feeling to have some space. After a solid day's work and a good night's rest, I'd get up nice and early and start house hunting again.

The Madrid travel assignment was a breeze. I wished I was taking some of the exotic voyages I described by rail. I kept picturing myself traveling with Jake. Jake and his twink.

I forced the thoughts of him from my mind. In the late afternoon, I drove over to Crossroads mall and remembered the wonderful night I'd had there with Jake. It seemed so long ago. I didn't think I could ever eat there again.

Finding food and comfort at Tony's Greek Taverna, I took an outdoor table and over a delicious chunk of pasticcio and a Greek salad, I bid on and won a new assignment. Now I was going to educate the expectant masses on the wonders of *How to Tie a Tie*.

My head clunked against the glass-topped table in the courtyard.

It could only happen to me.

I know how to tie a tie, a voice inside me said.

I laughed. It was a good thing that one of us did.

Where was my cock ring?

I felt in my pants and remembered it was at the motel room. I settled my bill and returned to the motel, anxious to lay my hands on that thing again. It was there in the zippered pocket of my leather jacket. I didn't feel horny. I wanted the power the ring gave me. I held it and waited. No power.

My mojo was gone.

I fell asleep, awakened by my cellphone ringing. It was James. I was so pleased to hear from him. He and my brother had crawled out of bed long enough to worry just a little about me.

"Where are you staying?" he asked.

"Malibu Shores."

"Oh, that's a nice motel. Let's hook up tomorrow, okay?"

"Well, I need to find a place to stay, but we'll talk, yeah?"

"I want to help you look. I'm still your best pal, right?"

"Right."

We ended the call and I felt a little better. I didn't feel like writing or watching the big plasma TV. I took a walk along PCH and stared at the ocean. Maybe I should have taken the place with the burned out kitchen.

No, it was ugly.

Thank you, Rafael.

I walked all the way down to Duke's, the Hawaiian restaurant, and sat on a stool in the Barefoot Bar. Everybody was watching a news report on the rat house on PCH.

"Authorities say over three thousand vermin had nested in the dead man's room and under the house."

Oh. My. God. I was gonna be known as the rat guy of Malibu. Mel Gibson had nothing on me. He had a potty mouth. My *life* was a potty. Now Jake would stay away from me for good.

"How the hell did these people live in that house and not know there was a dead guy and all those rats?" somebody asked the bartender.

My neighbor was dead? No wonder I hadn't seen him. I skipped the drink, not that anyone even noticed I was there. I walked back to the motel. Maybe I could live with a char-broiled kitchen. Especially if it was cheap.

At the motel, I sprinted up the stairs, surprised to see Jake pacing the front porch, muttering into his cellphone.

"He's here," I heard him say. He came over to me, his arms pulling at me. His face was so grim, I wondered what was wrong.

"Which room are you in?" he asked.

I was so happy, so overwhelmed to see him I couldn't speak. I handed him my room key. He took my hand since I didn't move, and he pulled me along with him.

We got inside the room and he threw me on the bed. I didn't care where he'd been, or with whom. I was just glad he was back. He shredded my T-shirt trying to get at me. I tore at his clothes as his tongue went from my mouth to my ass to my cock. He licked every inch of me.

"I'm so fucking mad at you," he said, between kisses.

"You're mad at *me*? Why?"

"Why didn't you tell me you were in trouble? I had to see it on the news!"

"What was I supposed to say? 'Hello, I have rats?'"

"No, you were supposed to say, 'I love you even though you're an ass and I want to live with you.'"

I laughed. "I don't think I would have thought of that."

"Yeah. I know." He slapped my ass. "Get on your knees."

He sucked my ass and it was wonderful. His fingers shot to my nipples, twisting and squeezing them. I braced myself as he reached down, took my hard cock and pulled it up toward him and he licked it from behind, paying some very nice attention to my balls. I kept reaching for his cock, but he wouldn't let me touch it.

"You'll get yours, rat boy."

He kept sucking and licking my back and legs.

"Did you screw the twink?"

"What twink?"

"From last night."

"I don't remember a twink. I woke up with a bottle of Jack Daniels."

He slapped my ass.

"Where are your rubbers?"

"Back home. You didn't bring them?"

"I only brought things I thought I'd need."

"And you really thought I'd stay away from you?"

His fingers stroked and poked at my ass.

"Can't you tell when a man likes you, Kris?"

"Um . . . yeah. I can tell."

"It's a good thing Daddy comes prepared, huh, rat boy?" He reached across the bed for his jeans and took a condom out of his back pocket.

I couldn't wait for him to slip it on and give it to me. Hard.

"Where's your cock ring?" he asked.

I reached across the floor for it. When I came back to the bed, he snapped it on me and put me on my knees again. He fucked me until I saw stars. I came so hard I couldn't hear him when he spoke. He turned me over, his cock still twitching inside me.

"Did you hear what I said?"

"I only want one cake."

"Okay." I smiled at him as he bent down to lick my cock.

"And this is me eating it." His mouth roamed my bound cock and balls. I felt Rafael chuckling inside me as Jake even tongued the cock ring.

Jake was so damned fucking adorable.

"You are my *tskheni*," he said.

"What the hell does that mean?"

"Horse. It's the only Georgian I know."

"Then ride me, baby. Ride."

He kissed me, taking my breath away.

It was better, so much better than cake.

ABOUT THE AUTHOR

A.J. Llewellyn is the author of over 250 M/M romance novels. She was born in Australia, and lives in Los Angeles. An early obsession with Robinson Crusoe led to a lifelong love affair with islands, particularly Hawaii and Easter Island.

Being marooned once on Wedding Cake Island in Australia cured her of a passion for fishing, but led to a plotline for a novel. A.J.'s friends live in fear because even the smallest details of their lives usually wind up in her stories. A.J. has a desire to paint, draw, juggle, work for the FBI, walk a tightrope with an elephant, be a chess champion, a steeplejack, master chef, and a world-class surfer. She can't do any of these things so she writes about them instead.

A.J. started life as a journalist and boxing columnist, and still enjoys interrogating, er, interviewing people to find out what makes them tick.

How to find/friend me:

email: ajllewellyn@gmail.com
website: www.ajllewellyn.com
www.facebook.com/aj.llewellyn
www.twitter.com/ajllewellyn
Newsletter sign-up: ajllewellynnewsletter@gmail.com—each month I give away a free ebook!
I'm an app! Download my FREE A.J. Llewellyn App for Android here: http://tinyurl.com/lkbc4wm